Floppy and the Bone

Written by Cynthia Rider

Illustrated by Alex Brychta

OXFORD
UNIVERSITY PRESS

Floppy saw a big bone.

"I want that bone,"
said Floppy.

So he took it!

"Stop! Stop!" said Biff.

"Drop the bone!" said Chip.

But Floppy didn't stop,
and he didn't drop the bone!

He ran up the hill.

He ran into a wood…

and onto a bridge...
and stopped!

Floppy looked down.

He saw a dog in the water.

The dog had a big bone.

Floppy wanted that bone, too.

Grrrrrrrr!
went Floppy.

SPLASH! went the bone.
SPLASH! went Floppy.

"Oh no!" said Floppy.

"The dog I saw was me!"

Why do you think Floppy took the bone?

What did Floppy see in the water? Did he think it was a real dog?

Do you think Floppy was a sensible dog in this story?

Have you ever wanted something as much as Floppy wanted his bone?

Picture puzzle

How many things can you find beginning with the same sound as the 'b' in ball?

Useful common words repeated in this story and other books at Level 2.

big dog he stop that the went

Names in this story: Biff Chip Floppy

(Answer to picture puzzle: ball, bike, bottle, bowl, boy, bush, butterfly)